GOOD MORNING ZOOM

A Goodnight Moon Parody
by Lindsay Rechler
Pictures by June Park

GOOD MORNING ZOOM

Written for Jack, Kenzie and all the children around the world.

Dedicated to our essential workers.

In your own living room
There was a computer and...
News that was gloom
Flowers in bloom
And a picture of-
All the kids from your class on Zoom

And there was your mom and dad
Working on their phones and iPad
And grandpas and nanas
At home waving to cameras
And again in our house
Mom's in the same pajama blouse

And out in the street you hear the sirens' call

And brave doctors and nurses helping us all

Good morning room
Good morning Zoom
Hello friends, I hope to see soon
Good morning light
And a world not quite right

Good morning indoor sports
And couch pillow forts

Good morning board game
And more of the same

Good morning rhyme
And hello screen time
Good morning grocery store
And packages at my door

Good morning sunlight
And goodbye fright

Thank you doctors and nurses
who will make things alright

Good morning air
And messy hair
Goodbye sirens everywhere

Good morning room
Good morning Zoom
Good morning world
I'll see you soon

Lindsay Rechler is a mother to two young children, Jack and Kenzie. She lives in Manhattan and is a Managing Director at a global investment bank. Like all parents, within the last few months, she and her husband Zack have also become chefs, bakers, coaches, teachers, musical directors, sanitizers, authors and artists.

This book was written for today's children and for future generations to record the impact the pandemic had on our lives and how we weathered the storm together.

For families staying home together.

Made in the USA
Middletown, DE
14 July 2020

12816617R00015